GEORGE THE FLYBOT
AND THE LOST CAMERA ON MOUNT EVEREST

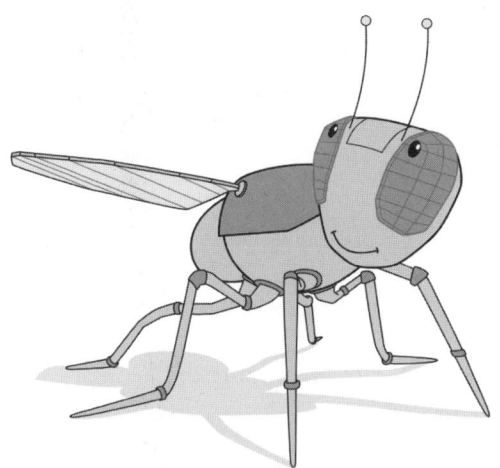

BY NESSA BELLIDO SCHWARZ
ILLUSTRATED BY JASON FRUCHTER

sunbird books
An imprint of PHOENIX International Publications, Inc.
Chicago • London • New York • Hamburg • Mexico City • Sydney

G.E.O.R.G.E.

FROM THE DESK OF
DARCY

SPECIAL DELIVERY
Battery Charger / G.E.O.R.G.E. User Guide

ATTN: Darcy Luna, Fly on the Wall Inc.

Please take care of our latest advancement in micro-robotics. GEORGE will be arriving tomorrow morning at nine o'clock sharp.

NOTE: Battery life is good for one mission at a time!

EVERYDAY ROBOTICS
SPECIAL EDITION · TECHNOLOGY · SCIENCE

BREAKING NEWS
FIRST ROBOTIC FLY RELEASED

Gadabout Enterprises has completed testing of a brand-new robotic fly. Its work could be far-reaching and history-changing. But is the world ready for a "flybot"? Headquartered in Boston, Massachusetts,

---

SCIENCE RESEARCH JOURNAL
Advanced Robotic Engineering

A Fly Like No Other

SCIENCE RESEARCH JOURNAL
Advanced Robotic Engineering

- Micro-wings
- Scanner
- Video camera
- Vision recept[or]
- Nighttime vi[sion]

TABLE OF CONTENTS

GEORGE's First Day........................... 4
Mission Log..12
Favel the Plateau Pika..........................20
The Growing-Up Years.........................28
Indie the Bar-Headed Goose....................36
No More Dillydallying..........................44
To Bother a Fox or a Yak.......................52
Khyber the Fox..................................58
A Glitch in the Programming...................68
What Does History Say?.......................76

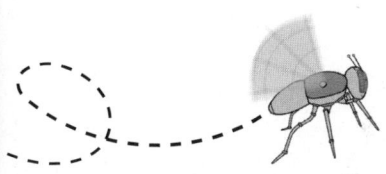

Chapter One
GEORGE's First Day

GEORGE the flybot flew over a pot of yellow daisies and hovered by the front steps of a three-story building, Fly on the Wall Inc. Tiny sensors sent a message to his robotic brain, which sent a message to his flight muscles: *Approaching human. Move or be squished.*

Faster than a human eye could track, GEORGE zipped to his left, avoiding a woman walking into the building.

She never even saw me, thought GEORGE. "Of course, nobody ever does," he whispered to himself as he flitted inside. To a human ear,

his whispering would have sounded soft and low, like a ripple of chimes fading in a breeze.

But being so tiny is why Fly on the Wall Inc. hired me in the first place, I suppose. Still, GEORGE was glad to have a new job. *Now if only I had a friend,* he thought as he landed on the desk of his new boss, Darcy Luna.

Darcy had large eyeglasses. They sat on the crook of her nose as she examined GEORGE with a magnifying glass.

"So you're the new microbot?" she asked, shuffling paper across her desk. "Ay! Now where is that battery port?"

GEORGE shivered straight down to his power actuators. Had he already done something wrong? Was he supposed to have brought a battery port from the university?

Was Darcy mad at him? Human moods could change without warning.

Humans = scary, GEORGE thought.

Darcy looked away and swept aside a pile of paper clips, a small metal screwdriver, and a stack of empty candy wrappers. At last, she retrieved a little black box from the cluttered mess.

"There you are, you old whapsadoodle!" she said.

The front of the box said GEORGE, and on the back of it were these words:

Geo

Engineering

Office of

Robotics at

Gadabout

Enterprises

"G-E-O-R-G-E. Ah, brilliant!" Darcy said. She sent GEORGE into the battery port to charge. "Five minutes and you'll be ready for your first mission. You'll be searching for a lost and super-important historical item from 1924. Exciting, huh, Georgie?" she said with a chuckle. "May I call you Georgie?"

GEORGE nodded as the electric charge from the battery port tingled down his spine, but his brain was still stuck on the word whapsadoodle. He searched his digital dictionary. Nope. No such word existed.

Maybe whapsadoodle is a human slang word that means something really valuable and important, GEORGE thought.

Five minutes later, Darcy said, "Before I program you for your first mission, I must give you an important warning."

As GEORGE undocked from the battery port, his antennae perked up.

"Don't fly too close to people," said Darcy. "Especially babies and grumpy gardeners."

I'm listening! GEORGE thought.

"Babies have chubby arms that swing without warning," Darcy continued. "And grumpy gardeners love flyswatters. The last thing we want is to damage your electronics."

An organic housefly had once warned GEORGE about the scary swatter.

The fly said: *swatter = death.*

GEORGE definitely didn't want that! He nodded in agreement.

Darcy programmed GEORGE for his first mission. Despite warnings of swatters swimming around his electronic brain, he felt a wave of anxious excitement, giving him goosebumps to the tips of his antennae.

What a curious feeling, GEORGE thought.

He had felt this way only one other time— on the day he was activated. Instead of eyes, GEORGE had vision receptors with dozens of lenses. When he'd opened them for the very first time, an intern was smiling down at him.

The intern took a deep breath. "I'm not sure I should do this," she whispered. "But you can't solve human problems unless you can *feel* things." Then she downloaded data into GEORGE's microcomputer. Something stirred deep inside his robot brain. "*Now* you're ready, little flybot."

That was GEORGE's first memory.

Now he had a new mission. And maybe if he was lucky—although he usually wasn't—on this new mission he would find a friend.

Organic houseflies had parents and siblings. GEORGE didn't even have that. If he made a friend, he wouldn't be lonely anymore. Being alone was for the birds. And GEORGE was a robotic fly—a one-of-a-kind flybot—*not* a bird.

Chapter Two
Mission Log

"Good luck!" Darcy Luna shouted as GEORGE flew out the open office door. "And stay warm!" He glided swiftly down the twisty hallways. In front of the building, sunshine filled the sky. Thin rays of light fell through the waving branches of a tall oak tree.

The warmth of the sun soaked into GEORGE's metallic body. And the sad thought that had been stuck to him like flypaper—*I'm all alone in the world*—began to fade a little. Just a little.

GEORGE's micro-wings, which were lighter than the lightest feather, began to flap quickly. Then all at once...*BZZZZZZZ!* He shot off into the sunlit sky toward his first mission, at 500 miles per minute.

Oh, my! So. Dizzy.

GEORGE had been dizzy when the interns at the university did a test run on his flight speed, too. *Not a bad dizzy,* he thought now, *but kind of like the way humans describe riding a roller coaster.*

The tiny GPS sensors on his antennae told him to fly east. Staying high enough to avoid airplanes, and low enough to avoid satellites, he zipped through the atmosphere like a miniature bullet train.

GEORGE squinted his vision receptors. They helped him to see light and color in higher definition than humans could.

So gray, he thought. *Now, blue.* Then a white cloud mixed with specks of sunlight swirled around him, like tiny golden ballerinas dancing in a powder of snow.

GEORGE gulped. *So beautiful.*

Seconds later, his body shivered. Fat drops of rain splashed off his back. Icy pellets of sleet slapped his face. *I need windshield wipers,* GEORGE thought as he raced through the misty clouds.

To keep his mind off the cold, GEORGE reviewed his mission log:

```
DESTINATION: Mount Everest,
   Himalayan Mountain Range.
MISSION TARGET: Small vest-pocket
   camera.
CAMERA LAST SEEN: With climber
   Andrew Irvine.
MISSION DETAILS: Andrew Irvine
   climbed Mount Everest with
   partner George Mallory in 1924.
   They never made it back down the
   mountainside. If the lost camera
   is found, and the film is
   developed, the photographs could
   change history.
```

Andrew Irvine (left), George Mallory (right)

pocket camera

Mount Everest

"I could change history," GEORGE said, amazed. He downloaded more details from his microcomputer:

The first climbers to reach the summit of Mount Everest and return were Edmund Hillary and Tenzing Norgay in May 1953.

GEORGE's electronic brain sorted through the facts. "If Irvine and Mallory reached the summit in 1924, then they got there before Hillary and Tenzing in 1953. So, who was the first to really reach the top? It's my mission to solve this human mystery."

Just then, his internal GPS went *BEEP-BEEP-BEEP* and gave a short *CHIRP.*

"I made it!" GEORGE shouted. "I flew 7,378 miles from Boston to Mount Everest in less than 15 minutes. Not bad, I think."

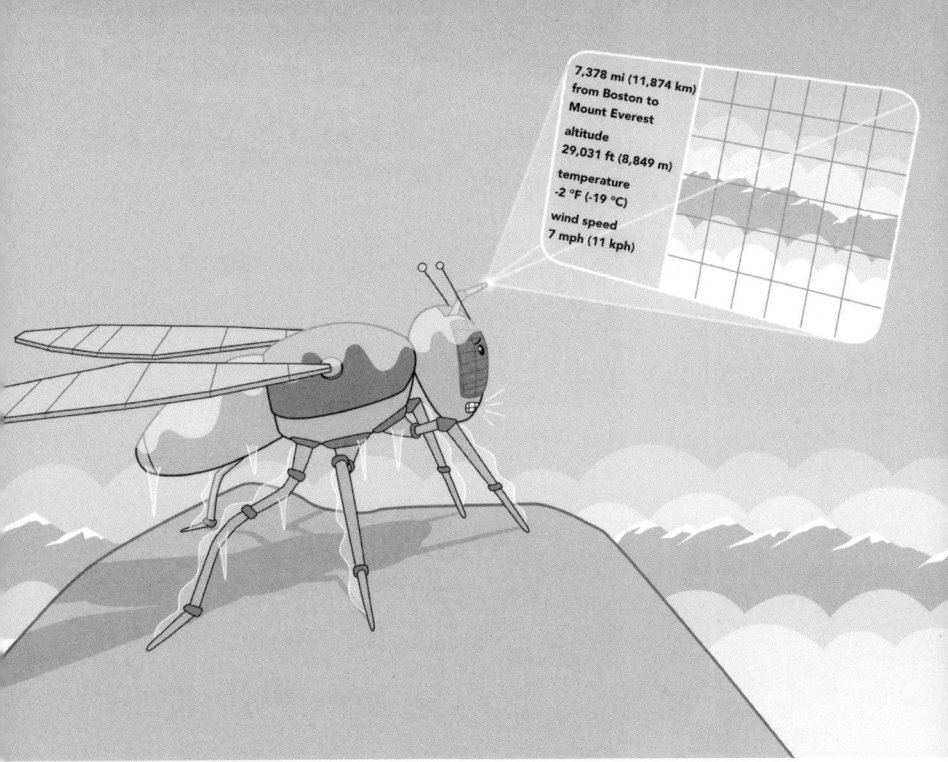

GEORGE made a steep turn downward to land on the mountain. A layer of frost coated his tiny metal body.

So cold, he thought. *No chubby babies with swinging arms or grumpy gardeners with flyswatters up here, that's for sure!*

Chapter Three
Favel the Plateau Pika

The snowy mountain sparkled in the sunlight, as if tiny stars had fallen to the ground. Giant boulders rose from the surface. Patches of grass, shrubs, and evergreen trees lined the rocky slopes and meadows below.

GEORGE activated his scanners. He was programmed to look inside small holes and crevices, where drones and humans had a difficult time reaching.

He landed on a mossy rock that had many hidden spots to explore.

GEORGE stretched his wings and rubbed his front limbs together. *Yes, perfect. A good place to start.*

A shadow moved as something scurried by. *Huh?* GEORGE's antennae stood up. *What's that?*

A small creature peeked out from behind a rock. It was about the size of a hamster GEORGE had once seen in Boston. Its pale brown fur ruffled in the strong wind.

"Hello," GEORGE said. "Who are you?"

The creature gazed at GEORGE with black beady eyes.

GEORGE stared back.

After what seemed to be a very long while—although GEORGE checked his internal clock, and it was only ten seconds—the creature replied timidly, "Oh, hi."

He spoke so quietly that GEORGE's global translator barely picked it up.

"Sorry. Having a hard time hearing you," GEORGE said. He adjusted the volume on his

audio sensors. "I'm GEORGE. What's your name?"

GEORGE's voice was fast and quivery. Why was he talking that way? Was it because he nervously hoped that the little creature might become his new friend? Maybe even his new best friend?

That was a lot to hope for from one tiny *Oh, hi*. But even so, GEORGE hoped. He just couldn't help but hope.

The creature looked down. "I'm Favel," he whispered.

GEORGE scanned Favel and downloaded some data:

MAMMAL: Plateau pika, a nonhibernating animal living on and around Mount Everest.
FACTS: Their cousins, the American pikas, gather grass to eat throughout the winter and burrow in the wintertime. But the plateau pikas survive year-round by using less energy in temperatures below 32 °F (0 °C). They stay alive by feeding on yak dung.

Yak dung = yak poo, GEORGE's digital dictionary told him.

Slowly, Favel started to inch back. But even as he scooched farther and farther away, his beady eyes stayed fixed on GEORGE.

"Don't go!" GEORGE called.

The pika stopped moving.

GEORGE flew closer to Favel, and in his kindest, softest voice he said, "Please don't be frightened. I'm trying to solve a mystery, and it would be nice if you might help me out."

Favel inched a little closer, which GEORGE took as a yes.

GEORGE smiled, which he had seen humans do as a sign of gratitude, but he wasn't sure Favel noticed.

"Many years ago," GEORGE explained, "two human males climbed this mountain. One of them had a pocket camera. If I find it, and the film is developed, we can solve the mystery about whether they were the first to reach the top. Would you like to see a photo of the camera?"

Favel shrugged with a small nod, which GEORGE took to mean: *I guess, if you really want me to.*

Chapter Four
The Growing-Up Years

GEORGE turned toward a tree and clicked on his micro-video projector. It shone a picture of a camera like the one Andrew Irvine had carried in his pocket.

"Have you seen this camera before?" GEORGE asked as Favel stared.

At last, Favel shook his head no.

"Oh," GEORGE said. "I was hoping that maybe you had."

"How did you do that?" Favel asked shyly.

GEORGE clicked off his micro-video

projector. The image disappeared. He clicked it back on and the picture reappeared. "You mean this?"

The pika's black eyes brightened as he nodded.

"The scientists who designed me included a projector to help me do my job. I make it turn on and off with a switch inside my brain."

"Scientists designed you?" Favel's voice rose, which GEORGE knew took a great effort, since pikas try to save energy in low temperatures. "Can you do lots of special things?"

GEORGE clicked off the micro-video projector. The image of the pocket camera disappeared again.

GEORGE had explained his beginnings to many organic flies and other insects during his first job, as a traffic monitor.

Their reaction had been similar to Favel's, which GEORGE decided was one reason he had such a hard time making friends. They didn't see him for who he was on the inside. They only saw his tiny gears and shiny switches, and all the things he could do.

Sadly, GEORGE realized that Favel would most likely *not* become his new best friend.

Still, he explained, "I was invented in a university laboratory by a group of scientists studying micro-robotics. A company called Gadabout Enterprises donated millions of dollars to the university. It took the scientists 22 years to build me."

"That's pretty neat," Favel said.

"Sure, I guess," GEORGE said. He honestly could not see what all the fuss was about. "After I was created, students called interns did a lot of experiments on me. That's the

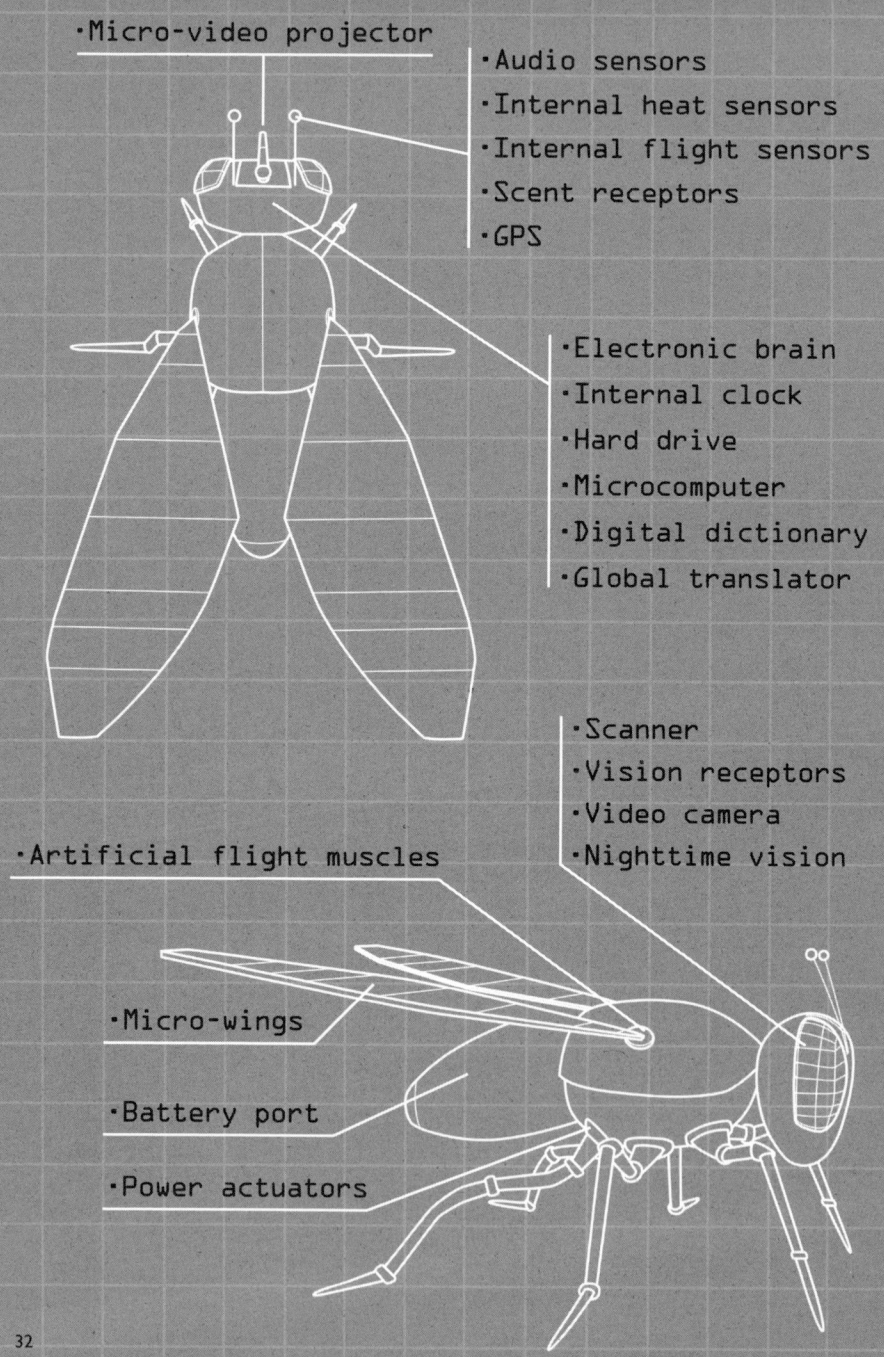

time in my life I call 'The Growing-Up Years.'"

He paused. "I didn't like that time much."

Favel nodded understandingly.

"After the interns got the bugs out—although I never understood that phrase, because I *am* a bug—I did traffic monitoring for a while. That was boring. But today, I'm on my first mission for Fly on the Wall Inc., to find the lost camera."

Favel asked softly, "Would it be all right if you showed me the picture again?"

GEORGE clicked on his micro-video projector, and the camera image reappeared.

While Favel gazed at the photo, GEORGE said, "The camera has been missing for a long time. It was last seen in 1924."

Favel tilted his head. "I think I remember something. The bar-headed goose who lives in the old dead tree once told a story about a camera. Maybe you can ask her about it. She lives that way."

With the tip of his black nose, Favel pointed south.

GEORGE turned to look. When he looked back again, Favel was gone.

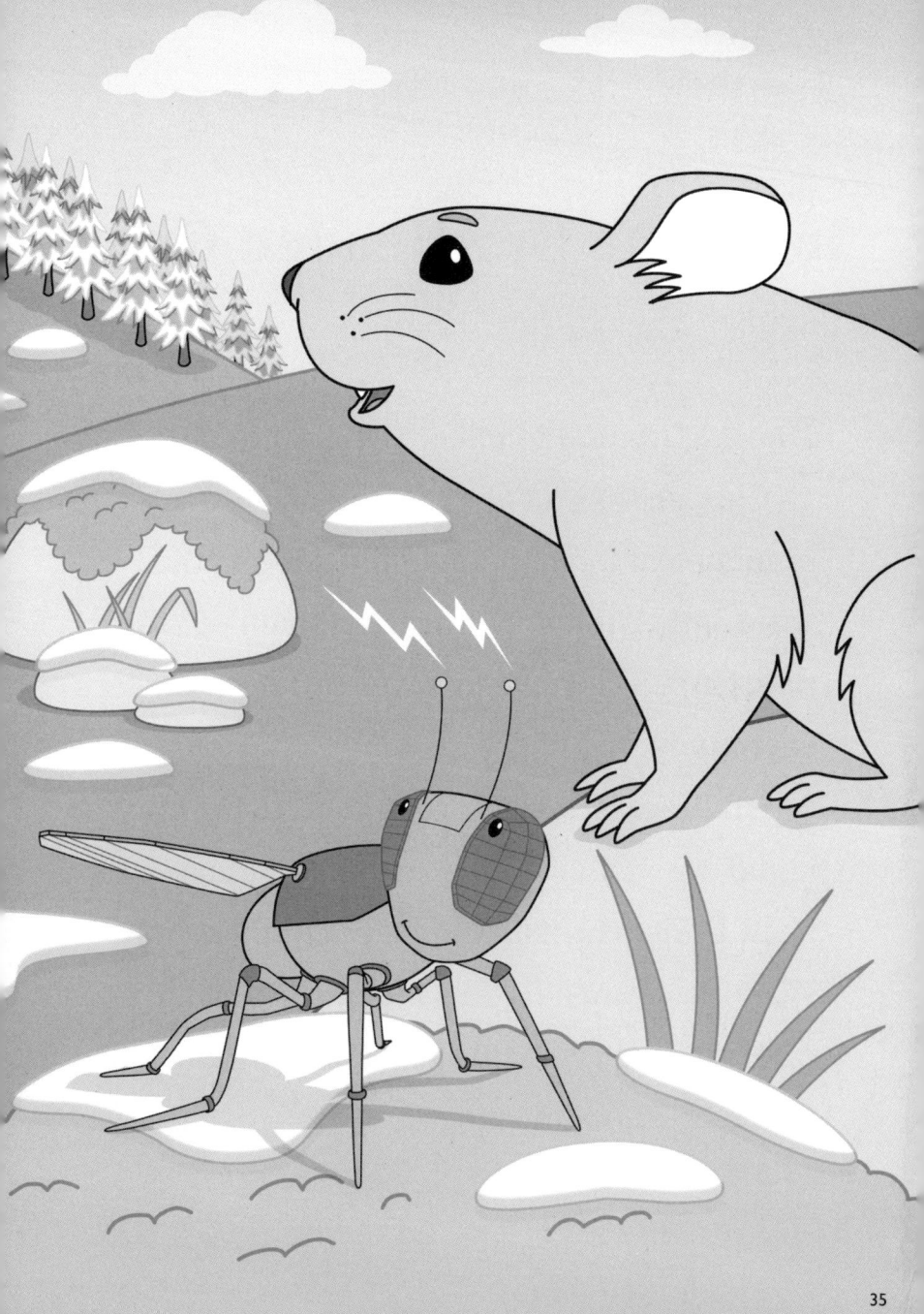

Chapter Five
Indie the Bar-Headed Goose

"Favel!" GEORGE called. "Where are you?"

Clusters of blue-green needles on the branches of a juniper tree fluttered in the wind. Other than the lingering smell of yak poo, there was no sign Favel had ever been there.

GEORGE scanned the ground using his nighttime vision sensor, which let him see heat. Under the surface, he could make out shadowy orange figures moving around.

Favel must have returned to his family, GEORGE thought sadly.

Family.

As he watched the shadowy figures scurry here and there, he wondered what it felt like to have mothers, fathers, brothers, or sisters. Sometimes, the interns would complain about their families. They would tell each other about the "big fights" they'd had with their parents and siblings.

But GEORGE had thought, *At least they are together. They are not alone, like me.*

He clicked off the micro-video projector and the nighttime vision sensor. For a moment, he sat still on the mossy rock and gazed across the snowy meadow.

His internal automatic heat sensors

activated. *Hmm, the temperature is warmer lower on the mountain,* GEORGE thought.

"No more dillydallying!" he said.

At the university, the head scientist was always telling the interns not to dillydally. GEORGE's digital dictionary had defined it as wasting time or delaying.

I have a mission to complete. Time to find a goose who lives in an old dead tree!

Favel had pointed south. GEORGE's micro-wings began to flutter, and with a quick flittering zip, he flew south across the terrain in search of the bar-headed goose.

A cool wind blew on his face as he peered across the surface of the mountain. And there, amid a forest of junipers, one bare tree stood out.

"That must be it," GEORGE whispered.

He navigated down. The thin branches of the tall dead tree hung over the live junipers, like a gray storm cloud over a silvery blue-green sea.

GEORGE's sensors were alerted. He landed nearby, and with his scanner, his digital eyes swept over the tree.

On the far side of the trunk, a large figure sat on the jagged edge of a broken branch.

Is that a bar-headed goose? GEORGE wondered.

He flitted over and hovered, scanning the figure as he downloaded data from his microcomputer:

BIRD: Bar-headed goose, species of bird that migrates across the Himalayan Mountains.

FACTS: High in the mountains, the air is thin and low in oxygen, making it hard to breathe and hard for most birds to fly. Bar-headed geese use wind drafts to help them, and they can slow down their metabolism so they need less oxygen. Bar-headed geese need more time to lift themselves into the sky than any other bird on the planet.

"Who are you?" asked the bar-headed goose. It perched on the stump of the branch with its webbed feet. "More importantly, *what* are you?"

"I'm GEORGE," he replied, "a microbot on my first mission. A pika named Favel told me that you might be able to help me."

"Favel, huh?" The goose ruffled its wing feathers, which were white and black and patchy brown. "Skittish fellow, isn't he? Nice of him to recommend me. So, what did he recommend me for? My name is Indie, by the way."

"Hello, Indie," GEORGE said. "I'm on a mission to find a lost camera from the year 1924. It was carried by Andrew Irvine, who climbed this mountain with George Mallory. If I find the camera, and the film is developed, the world will know whether they were the first climbers to reach the top of this mountain. Human history could be changed."

Indie clapped her wings together. "Bravo! Wonderful speech. Very moving." She bobbed her white feathery head.

GEORGE liked looking at the black stripes around Indie's eyes. But he was confused. "Thanks for saying so. But it's not a speech. These are facts. Do you know anything about the lost camera?"

"Do I know anything about it?" Indie opened her orangey-yellow beak and laughed a big booming *HONK! HONK! HONK!*

"Young fellow, I have flown to the heights of this mountain and beyond. There is nothing I don't know about it. I know about your frozen climbers from the year 1924. And I know where your lost camera can be found!"

Chapter Six
No More Dillydallying

"You know where the camera is?!" asked GEORGE.

"I do. But it won't be easy to get it," Indie warned. "You can find it in—"

BUZZ! BUZZ! BUZZ! went GEORGE's communicator. His internal audio activated.

"Georgie!" The voice of Darcy Luna boomed in his antennae. "Just checking in."

GEORGE sighed. *What awful timing!* He lowered the volume.

Darcy continued, "I've been watching

your video camera. And it seems you've gone off track. The video screen I am monitoring shows you hanging around—" She paused for a moment, and then added, "Yes, first a mammal, a plateau pika. And right now you're looking at, um, a bar-headed goose?"

Oh, drat, GEORGE thought. *I forgot about the video camera.*

He clicked off the monitor.

"I saw that!" Darcy said. "Turn that camera back on, Georgie." She mumbled under her breath, "Ay! I thought we had all these bugs worked out."

It's not a bug, GEORGE wanted to say. *It's just me doing my mission, like you programmed me to do.* But he couldn't communicate with Darcy without turning the camera back on. And right now, he had a goose to talk to.

Meanwhile, Indie gazed at him curiously.

"What's going on?" she asked.

GEORGE landed on a nearby branch.

"My boss is wondering why I'm dillydallying. But I'm not. I'm just finding the lost camera my own way."

Indie nodded. "Humans. Strange bunch! These days, they hike up and down the mountain, even though it's dangerous, and they leave trails of rubbish behind. Tents, coolers, pots and pans, you name it."

GEORGE shook his head. "I noticed that. Sometimes, I don't understand humans. Well, lots of times I don't."

He realized that he had not heard anything

more from Darcy Luna. Most likely, she was trying to work out the "bugs." GEORGE's video camera remained off, so at least Darcy couldn't see that he was still talking to the goose.

Indie rustled her feathers and tilted her head. "Listen, young fellow. Let me give you a bit of advice. Don't worry about trying to understand humans, or anybody else. Just learn to understand yourself, deep down."

GEORGE's vision receptors narrowed. Indie wanted him to figure out who he was on the inside? The part that others didn't see?

"Well, anyhoo," continued Indie, "about that lost camera. It was found by the

great-great-great-great-great-great-great-great-great-great-granddad of a local fox named Khyber."

GEORGE computed. "Ten! That's a lot of *greats*!"

"Yes, the camera has been in his family for many generations," Indie said. "Khyber the Fox—that's what he likes to be called—will not let it go easily."

"How do I find him?" GEORGE asked.

Indie raised her small black eyes toward the horizon. "His den is under the largest boulder between two deep valleys, down the far side of the mountain."

"Thank you for your—"

Just then, Darcy came back on the audio monitor. "Georgie, if you can hear me, please stand by. We're working on your video camera. I'm sure we'll get this bug worked out soon."

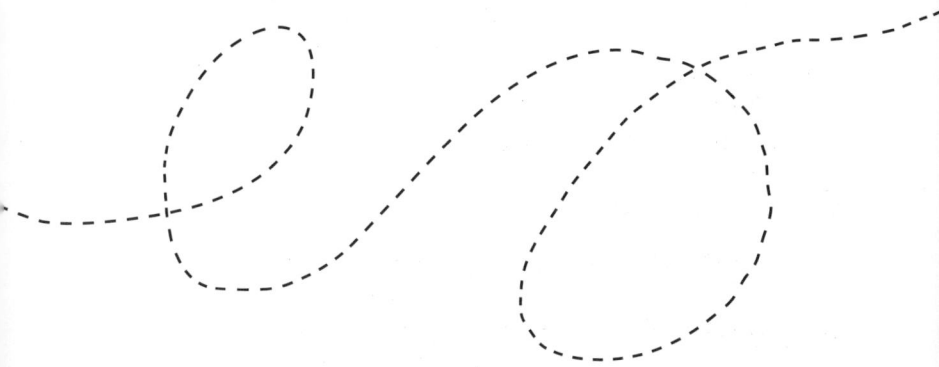

Chapter Seven
To Bother a Fox or a Yak

GEORGE said goodbye to Indie. Then he lifted off into the sky to the sound of her *HONK, HONK, HONK!*

His global translator reworded each *HONK* as *May you find a strong wind to carry you home!*

That's nice, GEORGE thought. *But I'm not going home yet. My mission has not been completed.*

As he soared over the mountaintop, he thought about home.

GEORGE had never had a home. Was Fly on the Wall Inc. his home now? Humans didn't live in office buildings. They worked in them. Who lived in an office building?

Just GEORGE.

He brushed that glum thought aside and wondered if he would ever see Indie again. He hoped so. She may not have become his best friend. But she certainly was friendly.

Within a few minutes, GEORGE saw a deep valley. The two mountains on either side looked like slides in a giant's playground.

"There it is!" he shouted.

In the middle of the valley was a huge boulder, just as Indie had said.

GEORGE landed on it.

"All I need is a photo and the GPS location of the camera," he reminded himself.

Fly on the Wall Inc. had a team to retrieve the camera and develop the film. GEORGE just had to get close enough to take a picture.

GEORGE downloaded data about the fox he was going to meet:

```
MAMMAL: Tibetan sand fox, living
    in high elevations of the Tibetan
    Plateau, usually north of
    the Himalayas.
FACTS: Their dens can be found near
    boulders and hilly terrain, away
    from thick underbrush and humans.
    Between hunts, they care for
    their young and rest in their
    dens. They also use their dens as
    a safe place to stay when they
    feel frightened.
```

He began to realize that Khyber the Fox was...a fox. With sharp fox teeth. And foxes were hunters. GEORGE wasn't sure if foxes hunted organic flies or flybots. But he was pretty sure a fox wouldn't be his friend.

With his long-range camera eyes, GEORGE scanned the area. He didn't see any foxes, but several hundred feet away, a wild yak stood among tall, dry grasses. Every so often, with

her lower teeth, the yak pulled up a clump of grass at its root. Then, with her long tongue, she stuffed the grass into her mouth, like a human licking an ice cream cone.

She sure makes it look delicious, GEORGE thought. *Hmm. Maybe I should ask that yak if she knows Khyber the Fox.*

With his wings purring at a low speed, GEORGE flew toward the yak. As he glided over the surface of the hill, he downloaded some quick data on yaks—*yaks are known to flee if approached.*

"Uh-oh," he said to himself. "Better to be safe than sorry!"

So, very quietly, GEORGE flew to one side of the yak. *Coming from the side will be way less startling than flying at her head-on.*

But just as he approached, the yak swung her long, bushy tail.

WHACK!

"*Aieeeeeee!*" GEORGE screeched as he tumbled across the grass.

Chapter Eight
Khyber the Fox

GEORGE opened his eyes. He was lying in the dirt by the large boulder. The sky and trees and hills were a blur. *What happened to me?* He shook his head and the world came into focus. "I remember now. No babies, no grumpy gardeners, but I still got swatted." He groaned. "Swatted by a yak."

He checked over his hardware.

Power actuators at maximum—*check*.

Internal sensors at maximum—*check*.

External sensors at maximum—*check*.

"I'm okay. I think," he whispered.

Suddenly, the eyes of a fox appeared above him. GEORGE launched into the air in surprise.

"What are you doing?" the fox asked.

GEORGE flew up to the fox's eye level and observed the dark outlines around its eyes.

"I'm GEORGE," GEORGE said. He hoped he sounded confident, even though he wasn't.

The fox said, "It appears as though you have been swatted by a yak. Are you all right?"

"I think so," GEORGE replied. "My internal hard drive seems to be working."

"Internal hard drive? Interesting. All over the mountainside, humans leave behind magazines and newspapers. You must be the one I read about, the only micro-robotic fly in the world."

Why did he have to bring up that awful word, "only"? GEORGE wondered. It made him feel so lonely.

"Yeah, sure," GEORGE said sadly. "That's me. One of a kind."

The fox nodded politely. "Khyber the Fox here. I'm honored to meet you, GEORGE. I read how you would be sent on missions all over the world. Splendid. What brings you to these parts?"

GEORGE explained his mission.

At once, the hairs on Khyber's neck bristled. "You will *never* get that camera!" he said with a growl. "My ancestors found it a hundred years ago, and they made it part of our den."

GEORGE squared his metallic shoulders. "My mission is to take a photo of the camera. That's all. My boss will send a team later to get it, but they only need the film. They want to develop the photos to see if Irvine and Mallory made it to the summit. I'm sure my boss will let you keep the camera, if you'd like."

He wasn't at all sure, actually. But he hoped she would.

"Humans are not to be trusted," Khyber said. "And if they remove the camera, my whole den will collapse. The den has been in my family for many generations. I won't let anything happen to it!"

"I'm sorry," GEORGE whispered. "I have no choice."

He activated his power actuators. And in the blink of an eye, he zipped past the fox and flew into the den.

Outside, he could hear Khyber growl. "Where did he go?"

Inside, GEORGE scanned the dimly lit den. Then he saw them.

Fox cubs!

The den was built of carefully balanced rocks, and right in the middle, three baby foxes slept in a fluff of fur and tails. Behind the sleeping cubs, the pocket camera was wedged tightly into the wall.

Every stone was necessary to hold up the fox's den...and so was the camera. Was it even possible for the Fly on the Wall Inc. team to retrieve the camera without making the rocks unstable? Even if they could, was it worth the risk?

GEORGE flew back outside.

The sun hung low in the sky. By a patch of berry bushes, Khyber the Fox sniffed about. He poked his nose up into the air and took a long whiff.

GEORGE hovered nearby, close enough to hear the fox mutter, "Micro-robots are difficult to track. He must be somewhere."

GEORGE landed on a berry. "I'm here!"

Startled, the fox looked up. "Where did you go?" he asked. "It's like you disappeared."

"I found the camera," GEORGE said, "and you're right. The camera is helping to support the base of the rock. If it's removed, your whole den will likely collapse." Another new and bothersome feeling—*dismay*—swept over GEORGE as he whispered, "I don't know what to do."

Khyber the Fox lowered his eyes. His

shoulders drooped. "I can't hunt you. I can't catch you. You're too fast. There is nothing to be done. If you bring humans back here, our family home will be gone." He looked at GEORGE. "What will you do?"

GEORGE rested his head on one metal limb. "If I don't take a photo of the camera and send the GPS location to my boss, I will be going against my programming. I'll fail my mission."

Khyber sat back on his hind legs. "Well, son, what do you consider failing? Is doing

the right thing failing?"

A blistering heat crawled up GEORGE's neck. He checked his internal heat sensors. *They seem okay*, he thought. *Why am I so warm?* Was this yet another unpleasant new feeling?

"I don't know." GEORGE's computer brain whirred and hummed and clicked. "I just… *don't know.*"

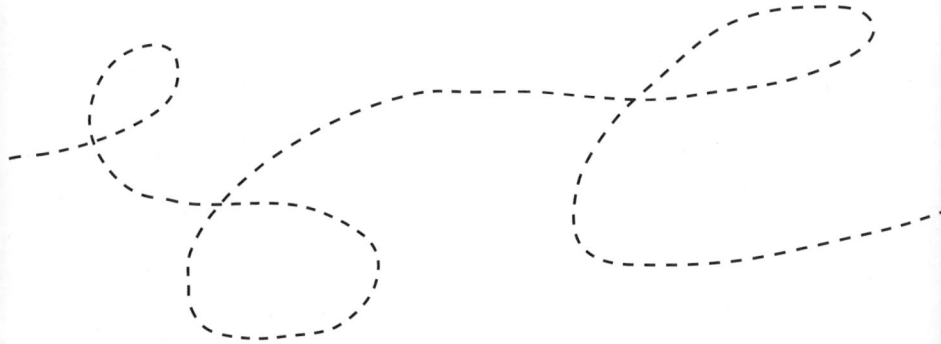

Chapter Nine
A Glitch in the Programming

GEORGE thought, and thought, and thought. He watched as the sun fell below the horizon and moonlight filled the sky. He breathed in the rich scent of ripe berries through his scent receptors. And at last, he knew what to do.

He'd actually known all along.

He looked into the sorrowful eyes of Khyber the Fox. And with a click, he switched his monitor back on and sent Darcy Luna a digital message:

MISSION ENDED: Search complete.
Returning to headquarters with no
data. Repeat: Departing mission
with no data to report.

GEORGE heard Darcy Luna shout, "The camera is back on!"

Her voice became muffled. She seemed to be speaking to someone else in the room. Then she said, "Georgie! I got your message. I'm glad that glitch has resolved. Too bad you couldn't find the camera. Signing off for now."

The expression in Khyber's eyes changed from sorrow to gratitude. "You're always welcome here," he said, and cleared his

throat. "My family is your family now."

GEORGE sniffled and nodded. He didn't know what to say. Was the fox only saying that to be polite? Or was it true? Did he, GEORGE the flybot, have a *real* family now?

GEORGE lifted into the sky. He rose higher and higher, and Khyber the Fox became smaller and smaller.

He flapped his wings faster. Then, in a flash, he bolted toward the fullness of the moon and into the starry night.

During the 15-minute flight, Darcy Luna sent him a message. "Before sending you out on your next mission, we're going to give your electronics a complete checkup. I'll see you soon at Fly on the Wall Inc. Safe travels, Georgie!"

She won't find anything wrong, GEORGE thought. *I'm just doing what Indie the bar-headed goose said I should do—finding out who I am, and being myself.*

A few minutes later, GEORGE's GPS went *BEEP-BEEP-BEEP, CHIRP.*

"I'm back!" he shouted. Because he was flying against the wind, it had taken a whole 17 minutes, but it didn't feel that long. GEORGE wondered why return trips always seemed to go faster.

He drifted down toward land. On Mount Everest, it had been nighttime, but here in Boston, it was midmorning.

Summer daisies were in bloom. Treetops swayed in a warm breeze. Birds flitted and chirped and danced between limbs and branches.

GEORGE stretched his wings and took in a deep breath. His antennae tingled pleasantly.

The warm sunshine felt good on his metal

body. He didn't miss the bitter cold of Mount Everest. But to his surprise, he did miss Favel the plateau pika, Indie the bar-headed goose, and most of all, Khyber the Fox and his newly found family.

GEORGE flew over Fly on the Wall Inc. Below, park benches lined the concrete sidewalk leading to the front door. On one park bench sat a young boy reading a book.

Very quietly, GEORGE hovered above the boy. The book he was reading had a lot of words. The boy turned the page. It had some interesting pictures too.

GEORGE saw that the boy had brown eyes. His eyes looked a little sad. GEORGE thought, *That boy looks like the way I feel. Is he lonely too?* Usually GEORGE's questions had answers that he could download. But this question was different, somehow.

As GEORGE flew toward the front door of the building, he wondered if Darcy Luna

would be disappointed in him. History had not changed—at least, not the way humans thought it would.

But Khyber the Fox and his family's history would be changed. They would have a safe home for many more generations.

As he glided down the twisty hallways toward Darcy Luna's office, GEORGE whispered to himself, "Yes, history has been changed...*exactly* as it should have been."

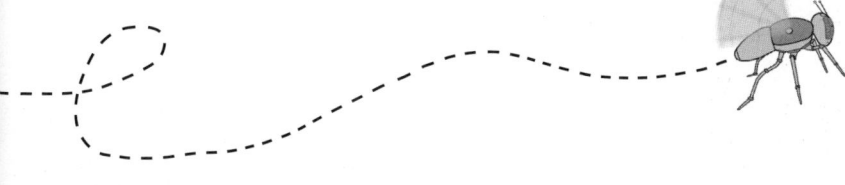

What Does History Say?

In the year 1924, climbing Mount Everest was considered nearly as hard as going to the moon. Two British climbers, George Mallory and Andrew Irvine, tried to do it anyway.

On Mount Everest, the air is so thin it is almost impossible for humans to survive the journey. Even at the level of Mallory and Irvine's base camp, 23,100 feet (7,041 meters) above sea level, humans struggle to breathe. Today, most people who try to climb Mount Everest have tools, thermal clothing, and other technology that did not exist when Mallory and Irvine set out 100 years ago. Yet, despite all the challenges they faced, they never gave up on their dream, making three different attempts to reach the peak.

Sadly, nobody knows if they made it up to the summit. The pocket camera in Andrew Irvine's coat has not yet been found.

Scaling Mount Everest—and standing for a few minutes on Earth's highest elevation—is a dream for many people. No matter the challenges and risks, climbers young and old come for the brief season when weather is clear and reaching the summit is possible.

Most people who come from around the world to climb Mount Everest need someone local to help them. Tourists hire experts called Sherpas to help them scale the dangerous mountain.

Mount Everest Firsts

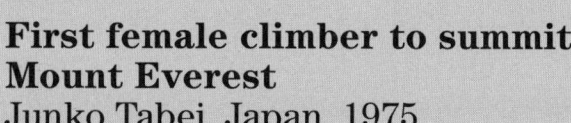

First female climber to summit Mount Everest
Junko Tabei, Japan, 1975

First solo climber
Reinhold Messner, Italy, 1980

First blind climber
Erik Weihenmayer, United States, 2001

Youngest climber
Jordan Romero (age 13), United States, 2010

Oldest climber
Yūichirō Miura (age 80), Japan, 2013

Most summits
28 times by Kami Rita Sherpa, Nepal, 2023

Nessa Bellido Schwarz is a Latina author who writes about history, science, nature, and the joys and perils of growing up. She lives in Southern California with her husband, her young son, and a tortoise named Leonardo da Vinci. Nessa is a longtime member of the Society of Children's Book Writers and Illustrators, and her work has been published in *Highlights* magazine. GEORGE THE FLYBOT is her debut chapter-book series for children.

Jason Fruchter is an illustrator and animator living his childhood dream. A graduate of the Rhode Island School of Design, Jason moved to New York City and worked for MTV Animation. Later, he cofounded A&J Studios, working with Cartoon Network, Disney, Nickelodeon, and Sanrio to illustrate popular characters for children. He now lives in Seattle, Washington, where he continues to draw well-known characters and create new character designs.

Published by Sunbird Books, an imprint of Phoenix International Publications, Inc.
8501 West Higgins Road   34 Seymour Street   Heimhuder Straße 81
Chicago, Illinois 60631   London W1H 7JE   20148 Hamburg

www.PhoenixInternational.com

Text © 2024 Nessa Bellido Schwarz
Illustrations © 2024 Sunbird Books, an imprint of Phoenix International Publications, Inc.

All rights reserved. No part of this publication may be reproduced or transmitted in any form or by any means, electronic or mechanical, including photocopying, recording, or any information or storage retrieval system, without prior written permission from the publisher. Permission is never granted for commercial purposes.

This book is sold subject to the condition that it shall not, by way of trade or otherwise, be lent, resold, hired out, or otherwise circulated without the publisher's prior consent in any form or binding or cover other than that in which it is published and without similar condition being imposed on the subsequent purchaser.

Sunbird Books and the colophon are trademarks of Phoenix International Publications, Inc., and are registered in the United States.

Library of Congress Control Number: 2024931810

ISBN: 978-1-5037-7225-0 Printed in China